Shocking Story
A baby on the doorstep cries…

"WHO'S MY DADDY?"

On Newsstands Now:

TRUE STORY
and
TRUE CONFESSIONS
Magazines

True Story and *True Confessions* are the world's largest and best-selling women's romance magazines. They offer true-to-life stories to which women can relate.

Since 1919, the iconic *True Story* has been an extraordinary publication. The magazine gets its inspiration from the hearts and minds of women, and touches on those things in life that a woman holds close to her heart, like love, loss, family and friendship.

True Confessions, a cherished classic first published in 1922, looks into women's souls and reveals their deepest secrets.

Shocking Story
A baby on the doorstep cries…

"WHO'S MY DADDY?"

From the Editors
Of *True Story* And
True Confessions

Published by True Renditions, LLC

True Renditions, LLC
105 E. 34th Street, Suite 141
New York, NY 10016

ISBN: 978-1-938877-75-9

Visit us on the web at www.truerenditionsllc.com.

Chapter 1

I looked up from my magazine as my next door neighbor, Gillian, came through the front door without knocking.

"Samantha, do you have any birthday candles?"

It was on the tip of my tongue to ask her what she thought I'd be doing with birthday candles since I didn't have any kids, but I stopped myself in time. What was the use? I knew that Gillian wasn't being deliberately insensitive. Besides, I did have candles, but only because Tracy, my husband, had insisted on turning my last birthday cake into a dangerous inferno.

In the end, the melting candles had ruined the cake and we discovered our fire extinguisher needed to be replaced. Not exactly a romantic moment, but I guess it was the thought that counted.

"Yeah," I said, returning to my magazine. "In the second drawer to the left of the dishwasher. Help yourself."

"Oh, thanks." Gillian disappeared into the kitchen and returned a few moments later with the box of candles. "Don't forget, party's at two o'clock in the park."

I looked at her with a lifted brow. "Forget? I'm glad you reminded me. You know, with my busy schedule it would be so easy to forget." My sarcasm got a smile out of her.

"Yeah, me, too. Oh, by the way, did you notice someone was looking at the Reed house today?"

The magazine article I'd been reading on reducing the clutter in your house was forgotten. When someone mentioned the Reed house, it was as if E.F. Hutton had spoken. I threw the magazine onto the sofa beside me. "Tell me everything," I demanded, all ears.

Gillian shrugged her dainty little shoulder while her eyes danced with mischief. "I don't want to keep you from your magazine."

"Gillian . . . ."

"All right. She looked young, maybe early twenties. Bombshell, from what I could see. Tall and blonde."

"That's it?" I asked, unable to hide my disappointment.

"Well . . . no. She was carrying something in a basket. She went in with it, but didn't come out with it."

My jaw dropped. This was news! "You think she bought the house?" If she'd gone in with something and had left without it, what other explanation was there? And what was the woman doing looking at the house without a real-estate agent?

"I don't know. Maybe Natasha will know something, or she can

1

ask Brandon. He's a real estate agent—he should know something." Gillian checked her watch. "Ooops! Gotta get going. I'll see you at the party."

"Yeah, see you there."

We called our cove "Widower's Circle," although it was officially named after Elliot Reed, the multimillionaire land contractor who originally bought the land and built the seven beautiful houses that made up the cove.

The reason we called Reed Cove something else entirely was that all the homemakers—myself included—felt like widowers most of the time. I was married to a dedicated doctor, Phyllis was married to a dedicated lawyer, Kara was married to a workaholic who owned a chain of restaurants, Gillian was married to a very successful business consultant who traveled often, Natasha's husband was a real-estate agent, and Sloan—well, we weren't certain what Sloan's husband did, but he was wealthy enough to buy a house in the cove and give Sloan basically anything she wanted.

Anything except his time. In that respect, Sloan was just like the rest of us. Lonely.

I mentioned seven houses and only six couples because the seventh and biggest house was vacant. It was a house that had once belonged to Elliot Reed and his wife. It had remained empty after four years. We called it the Reed house.

What happened in that house four years ago was common knowledge, and even Natasha's husband, who had often bragged he could sell a shack to a senator, had taken a crack at selling it and failed. The problem was that everyone knew the history of that house, and nobody cared to live with it. In fact, the thought of going inside the house gave me the creeps. Tracy, my physician husband, laughed at my fears, much to my chagrin.

Tracy and I had been in our new house in Reed Cove about three weeks when the tragedy happened. I remember thinking, as I watched the ambulance and numerous policeman pouring into the house and onto the surrounding grounds, that Tracy and I had made a mistake. If this was an indication of what life was like in the cove, maybe Tracy and I hadn't made the right choice in purchasing our house.

Yet, it was on that tragic night that I had a chance to get to know the other women of Reed Cove. They gathered in our yard—our house sat next to the Reed house—and without hesitation filled me in on the story behind Elliot Reed and his super model wife, Sloan. After brief introductions, each woman contributed to the story in such rapid succession it made me dizzy just listening to them.

"Elliot's wife of twenty years left him after catching him with that super model, Sloan." Natasha pointed to the covered body on the stretcher parked behind the ambulance. "That's Sloan, there."

Phyllis stepped closer, lowering her voice as if it mattered. "She was after his money, of course. Promised him kids. He and his first wife couldn't have any."

I remember thinking at the time that it must have been horrible not being able to have kids when you truly wanted them, never realizing that I would eventually know from experience.

"She got pregnant right away, and lost the baby before her fourth month," Kara added.

Sloan shook her head. "I don't believe she 'lost' it. I think she took something to make it happen."

By this time, my head was swimming as I looked from one to the other. Kara and Gillian agreed with Sloan, while Phyllis and Natasha had other ideas.

"No, I think the first time was a miscarriage," Natasha argued. "I saw her the next day, and she looked really sad."

"You always were a pushover, Gill," Sloan said, not unkindly. "If she was sad about losing the baby, why would she have an abortion later?"

"She—she—" But they weren't ready to let me speak, apparently, for I didn't get to finish my question.

"Yeah, she did. Bragged about it to all of us as if she'd done something grand and brave. She even talked about how torn up Elliot was over it, even though she'd told him that she'd had another miscarriage."

Finally, I was able to get a word in. "Wasn't she afraid he'd find out?"

Sloan grimaced. "We didn't like her much, but we wouldn't have ratted on her."

"Somebody did," Kara said gravely, staring at the scene.

"You think that's what happened, Kara?"

"Yeah, I do. I can see the blood soaking through the sheets from here. In any case, we'll know in a moment. I sent Luke to find out what happened."

"Luke's home?" Phyllis asked with a mixture of surprise and envy.

I think it was then that I started to feel as if I belonged. Tracy might as well have used the hospital as his home address since he lived there most of the time. I knew when I married him that he would be working a lot of hours as a doctor, but that didn't stop me from becoming lonely.

"He sliced his finger open on a chef's knife," Kara explained. "Had to have six stitches. He can't get it wet, so he's howling at the moon. Look, here he comes."

3

As I followed her line of vision, I caught sight of Luke cutting across the Reed yard in our direction. He was a tall, thin man with thick brown hair and blue eyes. His features were almost feminine.

"Murder-suicide," he told us breathlessly the moment he got within hearing distance. "Looks like Elliot shot Sloan in the stomach, then blew his own brains out afterwards."

We fell silent beneath the disturbing news. I hadn't known the Reeds, but I felt awful about what happened. What could drive a man to such lengths? Did Elliot Reed want a child so badly that he didn't want to live if he couldn't have one? Was his rage so great that he murdered his own wife, then shot himself? It was inconceivable to me that anyone could be that unhappy.

"Not a very nice welcome, Samantha," Phyllis commented as we all stood in our little group watching the scene. "But you'll be happy to know the rest of us aren't quite that neurotic."

Well, that's a relief, I thought.

Four years after the Reed tragedy, after numerous showings and drastic price cuts, someone had been seen carrying something inside the infamous Reed house . . . as if they were moving in.

Chapter 2

We were all beside ourselves with curiosity by the time Gillian's son's birthday party began. Instead of the usual chitchat about kids, clothes, husbands, and recipes, the conversation centered on the Reed house and who might be moving in.

The day was warm for mid-April, a spectacular day to have a birthday party in the small private park located in the center of our cove. The crowd consisted of the cove residents, and various members of Gillian's family as they gathered to celebrate Gillian's son's sixth birthday.

Sloan and Lee were practically newlyweds, having gotten married a year earlier after living together in the cove for a couple of years. The bachelor party the guys held for Lee was still something of a sore subject with the wives, even after a year, since the men were suspiciously closed mouth about the entire deal.

Phyllis and Drew had two girls, age's three and five. Natasha and Brandon were childless by choice, at least for the time being, and Kara and Luke had one daughter who was also six years old.

Tracy and I had been trying to get pregnant for the past two years. I was beginning to grow frustrated over our failure, but Tracy kept assuring me that it takes time. He was reluctant to start the endless rounds of fertility tests, and to tell you the truth, so was I. I think I was afraid of the results.

While the kids played on the park's playground equipment, we gathered around Natasha, who was talking to Brandon on her cell phone. I have to admit, by the time she hung up, I was about to pop.

"What? What did he say?" I demanded. My demand was echoed by the others.

Natasha frowned and shook her head. "He says that he's as stumped as we are. Real Estate agencies don't just give someone the key and let them wander around by themselves." She tapped the phone against her leg. "He's going to call the company and see what they say."

"And he's going to call you right back?" Phyllis asked, keeping one eye trained on her daughters. They were seated on the merry-go-around, hanging on for dear life as Sean, the birthday boy, pushed them at top speed.

We gathered around the picnic table, which Gillian and her mother had decorated with balloons and streamers, and sat down to wait for Brandon to call back. Gillian's mother knew the history of the

5

Reed house and was as curious as the rest of us.

"Maybe the woman you saw was an agent?" Gillian's mother asked, startling us all.

Why haven't we thought of that? I wondered, feeling foolish. "Of course!" I said. "That would explain why she was alone. She was probably dropping off some potpourri or something to spiff up the house before she showed it to a client."

Gillian bit her bottom lip and frowned. "She didn't look like a real estate agent. She was wearing tight leather pants and some kind of glittery cropped top that showed a lot of skin. And she had on red high heels."

I was amazed at Gillian's detailed observations and silently wondered if she'd been watching the woman through a pair of binoculars. The thought made me smile.

"Can you imagine someone buying the house after all this time?" Kara said, dipping up a cup of punch from the punch bowl on the table. She took a sip and smacked her lips. "This is good."

"I can't imagine anyone buying it knowing what happened inside." Sloan gave a delicate little shiver. "I know that I couldn't sleep in that house."

"I'm not even sure I could go inside," I murmured, glancing quickly around to see if anyone found my confession funny.

They all stared back at me solemnly, as if they all agreed.

Natasha's phone rang. I held my breath as she answered it.

When she hung up, she said, "And the plot thickens. Brandon said the agency didn't send anyone out, and that they haven't shown the house in weeks. He says they're going to send someone over to see if the woman did any damage to the place."

Gillian shook her head. "I don't think she was in the house long enough to do any damage. But she did leave something, and I'd like to know what it was."

I could see that we all agreed. We all wanted to know

"In the meantime," Gillian added, getting up, "Let's get this party on the road, shall we?"

Chapter 3

Two hours later, the party had wound down. The kids were getting cranky and bored with the playground equipment. I was beginning to think that the agency had changed its mind about sending someone out to check out the house when a car turned into the cove.

I watched in silence as the car drove past us and up the slight hill to the Reed house. A man got out, glanced our way, sighted us, waved, then disappeared inside.

"The suspense is killing me," Phyllis murmured.

"Mom, can we go inside and play video games?" Sean asked Gillian.

With an absent wave, she said, "Sure, sure. Go ahead. Just don't break anything." Gillian's mother volunteered to go with them and keep an eye on things.

"How long has he been inside?" Sloan asked.

I looked at my watch. "Five minutes so far."

"It's a big house," Natasha reminded us unnecessarily.

"He's not getting past us without telling us what was in that basket," Phyllis said.

"Damn straight he isn't," Kara said.

Together as a group, we moved from the luscious park grass to the asphalt drive that made a circle inside our cove. The real estate agent wouldn't get past us unless he mowed us down.

As it turned out, we didn't have to worry. The man came rushing from the house and toward us, obviously in a panic about something.

"Oh, God. What if it was a bomb?"

Leave it to Sloan to think of the worst possible thing that could happen! And now that she'd planted the idea, I immediately began to worry about the location of my own house next to the Reed house.

When the man reached us, I saw that he was young, maybe late twenties, and good looking. And he looked furious.

"Is this some sort of joke?" he demanded, raking his hand through his hair. I saw that his hands were shaking as he stared at each of us in turn. "Because if it is, I have to tell you that trespassing is against the law."

We were all dumbfounded by his words. Finally, it was Phyllis who found her tongue first. "Excuse me? You mind telling me what you're talking about? We're the ones that reported that woman going inside."

The poor man looked even more confused. "But—but—you mean she left?"

"Yeah," Phyllis said a little sarcastically. "We just want to know what was in the basket she left inside."

"Come on, I'll show you," he said, the panic returning. "I can't believe this is happening." He took off at a jog back up the slight hill to the Reed house.

Reluctantly—and I mean very reluctantly, we followed. When we got to the open door, everyone hung back. Nobody wanted to be the first to step inside.

"Come on!" the man shouted from inside the house. "I need your help."

Phyllis and I exchanged worried looks. Finally, I said, "Okay, I'll go first." It didn't look as if anyone else was going to volunteer. "But I'm not going alone." I felt silly, but I couldn't help it. Call me superstitious or paranoid or both.

Sloan shouldered the others aside. "I'll go with you."

"We might as well all go," Kara said. "If the man had found a bomb, I don't think he'd be encouraging us to come inside—and he wouldn't be inside either."

So, huddled together like a bunch of school kids entering a haunted house, we moved slowly into the large foyer.

"I'm in the kitchen," the man said, his voice echoing eerily.

Gillian took the lead. "I know where the kitchen is. Follow me."

Chapter 4

In the kitchen, the man was standing over a basket on the floor, shaking his head and mumbling. My curiosity finally overcame my fear; I stepped closer to look inside the basket.

I gasped, reeling back. One by one, the others took a look, each reacting the same way.

We were all stunned into silence.

The man looked at us, his expression dazed. "Told you it was shocking," he said, staring down at the basket.

I felt the strength leave my legs and grabbed the nearest arm—which happened to belong to Gillian. "It's a baby," I said in a strangled voice. "The woman left a baby alone in this house." I sounded more horrified at the thought of the baby being alone inside this particular house than I did over the woman's desertion.

"Maybe she plans to come back and get it," Kara suggested, but without much conviction.

"But why would she leave it here in the first place?"

It was a question that was on all of our minds, I think. The poor man gave his head a helpless shake. "What am I supposed to do? There wasn't anything in my training about what to do in a situation like this."

"Maybe there's a note or something," I said, creeping forward again. The baby was tiny, possibly three months old. Right now, it was sleeping peacefully all snuggled inside the wicker basket; oblivious to the many pairs of astounded eyes watching it.

Her, I thought, staring at the pink cotton sleeper. It was a girl. She had a pacifier in her mouth, and every so often, she would suckle in her sleep. I reached out and twitched the receiving blanket aside.

There was an envelope tucked against the baby's side. Conscious of the murmurs of awareness around me, I plucked the envelope up and opened it, withdrawing a sheet of stationary.

"'Who's my daddy?'" I read aloud. Phyllis gasped. Sloan covered her mouth with her hand. Heart pounding, I read on. "'To the snots of Reed Cove—you figure it out. I leave you one clue.'"

"Well, what's the clue?" Kara demanded, trying to snatch the note from my hand. "She called us snots. Is she talking about us?"

I moved it out of reach, my gaze going to the bottom of the page. There was a date. I read the date aloud.

Sloan shrieked. "That's the day before my anniversary!"

A stone-cold silence fell. The agent, looking very confused, regarded us as if we were all lunatics.

Finally, Gillian said what I felt certain was on everyone's mind. "The bachelor party. That's the day of Lee's bachelor party."

Kara sounded faint as she added, "The party none of the guys will talk about."

"Lee claims he doesn't remember anything."

"Drew," Phyllis said, "claims he doesn't know how those crotchless panties wound up in his pants pocket."

"Tracy had . . . had glitter on his . . . his—" I snapped my mouth closed, suddenly, remembering there was a stranger among us.

Apparently, Gillian didn't care. "After that party, Gage didn't make love to me for a month. Said he was tired."

"Oh, God," Sloan moaned, covering her face. "Is this woman—this woman trying to imply that this baby belongs to one of our husbands?"

After a long, staggering silence, I said, "I think that's what she's saying. I think she's also saying that she doesn't know who the father is, either."

"What a tramp," Phyllis spat.

Without thinking, I stopped her before she could light it. I nodded at the baby. Phyllis frowned, but put the pack back inside her purse. "She called us 'snots' as if she knew us."

"We can probably thank our better halves for that," Kara said tightly. "Wonder why she left the baby here, of all places? Why not just on someone's doorstep?"

"If she did that," Gillian pointed out, "Then that would imply that she knows who the father is. I don't think she does know, and this way is more dramatic. She's probably scheming to milk us all for every penny she can get."

The baby let out a soft sigh in her sleep. We all focused on her. Something fuzzy and warm curled around my heart. Whomever she belonged to, she was first and foremost a baby.

I felt a very strong anger toward the baby's mother. How could the woman just leave her baby here, alone, in this house? What if someone hadn't found her? She couldn't have been absolutely certain someone had seen her bring the basket in, could she? Not unless she knew of Gillian's penchant for spying on her neighbors. Not much got past Gillian, and, subconsciously, I had come to depend upon her to keep me informed.

"What am I supposed to do about the baby?" the agent asked in a bewildered voice. He obviously had trouble following our conversation.

"We'll take care of her," I said, surprising myself. "I'll take her to my house."

"Why don't we all adjourn there so that we can talk about this?" Sloan suggested.

I could tell that Sloan was struggling not to cry, and I knew exactly how she felt. "Yeah, let's all go to my house. Gillian, why don't you see if your mother will stay a little longer and watch all the kids at your house?"

"Yes, I'll ask her, then I'll be right over."

Very carefully, I gathered up the basket and the envelope and together we left the Reed house. I, for one, wasn't sorry to be leaving that creepy place.

Chapter 5

At my house, I set the sleeping baby on the kitchen table and made coffee. I think we were all reluctant to say anything until Gillian joined us.

Finally, when we gathered around the table with the baby in the middle, I began our discussion. "I think we should start by trying to remember everything that we can about the night of the bachelor party, and I think we should start with who hired the stripper. Did we ever find out?"

After a brief silence, Natasha raised her hand. "I didn't tell anyone because I didn't want you to be mad at Gage. Believe me, I was mad enough for all of us."

"Did he say how he knew her?" I asked gently. Shamefully, my heart leaped with anticipation. I remember thinking how much I wanted the fault to lie with Gage instead of Tracy. I could hardly bare the thought of Gage sleeping with another woman. I imagine the others felt the same.

"He said a client recommended her."

I let out a sigh. "At least we should be able to find out her name."

"If she used her real name," Phyllis said with a snarl.

Natasha kept her gaze on her coffee cup as if she couldn't bear to look at us. "Gage said it was just a little bit of harmless fun, that the stripper wasn't a hooker or anything, and that they weren't even allowed to touch her."

The baby, as if to remind us all that she was living proof that Gage had lied about the facts, let out a tiny cry, then settled into sleep again.

"Somebody did some touching," Sloan whispered. She was crying silently, and I wondered if she was even aware of it.

"Tracy was pretty wasted when he got home," I said, glancing around the table. Almost as one, they all agreed that their husbands were drunk. "So they were all drunk."

"What does that tell us?" Kara demanded.

She had a good point. The problem was, I didn't know the answer. "I'm just trying to assimilate the facts, Kara."

"No matter how many times I've asked him," Sloan said, "Lee continues to say he doesn't remember much about that night." She hesitated, then added, "He thinks one of the guys slipped something into his drink."

Suddenly, everyone was staring at me. Because Tracy was a doctor, I realized, flushing beneath their expectant gazes. Still, I found it hard to believe that Tracy would be so reckless . . . especially knowing that Lee was drinking. I shook my head. "No, Tracy wouldn't do it. He won't even let me take Tylenol if we've been drinking."

"This was a bachelor party, Samantha," Phyllis reminded me gently.

I wanted to reach across the table and slap her, and the urge stunned me. I knew that we would have to be very careful that we didn't end up pulling each other's hair out. This was a very, very serious situation, and I knew that it could easily get out of hand.

Squaring my jaw, I repeated, "I don't think Tracy would mix drugs with alcohol. He knows the dangers."

Sloan came to my rescue. "Samantha's right. I think Tracy would be the last person to do it."

"If anyone did it in the first place," Natasha said, staring at Sloan defiantly. "Lee thinks someone might have doctored his drink. Isn't it just as likely that he drank too much?"

Another big tear slipped down Sloan's cheek, evoking my sympathy. I imagine that she felt the guiltiest because it had been her husband's bachelor party.

"Yes, it's likely, Natasha," Sloan said. "Thanks for pointing that out for me."

I could sense the temperature rising in the room and sought to cool it. "Can anyone at this table say without a smidgen of doubt that this baby couldn't possibly belong to your husband?"

Just by looking at each of their faces, I knew that nobody would raise their hand. Not a single one of us was that confident in our marriages or of our husbands. Oh, we might silently tell ourselves that we didn't believe it could happen, but none of us could say the words aloud.

Including me. I couldn't forget that suspicious sprinkling of glitter on his penis, although Tracy claimed one of the guys had dumped the glitter down his pants just to get him into hot water with me. At the time, I had believed him because I'd had no choice.

Now . . . now I had to reconsider Tracy's explanation, just as Sloan had to reconsider Lee's convenient claim that he didn't remember much of anything.

That left Phylicia's husband, Drew, Gillian's husband, Gage, Kara's husband, Luke, and Natasha's husband, Brandon. The others seemed to realize this as well.

Phyllis sighed and said, "There's the panties I found in Drew's pants pocket."

"And don't forget that Gage wouldn't make love to me for a month afterward," Gillian said in a low, embarrassed voice.

Natasha looked at Kara, and Kara looked at Natasha.

Still staring at Natasha, Kara blurted out, "I found a feather."

"A feather?" I prompted when she didn't continue. I'd found glitter, but I had specified where I'd found it. Kara seemed reluctant to continue, and I was curious to know why. From the looks of the other expressions around the table, I wasn't alone.

So we waited.

Her voice so low I could barely understand her, Kara said, "In his zipper. It was stuck in his zipper. He doesn't know that I saw it."

Okay, I thought. The feather was as bad as the glitter, but it didn't necessarily mean either men had been unfaithful. But it was a strong possibility, even I had to admit that.

Natasha was left, and by this time, nobody was feeling any sympathy for the other. Maybe that was why she seemed so hostile. We soon found out another reason for her hostility.

"The kid can't be Brandon's," she snapped out. "Brandon doesn't like kids. Brandon doesn't want kids, so he wouldn't be careless." She lowered her eyes, but not before I saw tears sparkling there. "I should know. He never forgets to use a condom. He doesn't trust me to take the pill."

Her confession was shocking, mostly because she'd never talked about the subject before. I had always assumed they were waiting for the right time to have kids.

Chapter 6

Despite the fact that Natasha was obviously upset, Phyllis didn't hesitate to point out the obvious. "You said yourself that Brandon was drunk, Gill. He might have been careless. He could be the father."

"It would serve the bastard right," Natasha growled perversely, then burst into tears.

Comforting one another was the last thing on anyone's minded right then, so Natasha was left to suffer alone. But we were courteous enough to wait until she pulled herself together before we continued our discussion.

"So what are we going to do?" Sloan wanted to know.

She was staring at me, so I figured I had been unofficially nominated to head the group. I can't say that the idea made me happy or proud. I think I would rather have been on the moon. "I don't know about anyone else, but I think it's time Tracy told me the truth about what happened that night." There was a wave of agreement around the table. Inwardly, I cringed at the thought of finally hearing the sordid details of the bachelor party. It was easier to forget it ever happened.

But the baby reminded me that forgetting was no longer an option. It hurt, thinking that Tracy might be the father. I wanted a baby with Tracy. I wanted to be pregnant with Tracy. He was my husband, dammit.

As if aware that she was the object of my thoughts, the baby began to awaken. I leaned forward, holding my breath as I watched her squirm and wiggle and open her eyes.

And like all babies when they're first born, her eyes were a murky, dark blue. She must resembled her mother, I thought, reaching out to touch her tiny fingers as she flayed her hands about. Because she didn't look like anybody that I knew. She had blond hair—what there was of it, which was very little—and a round, chubby face. No telltale dimples or clefts in the chin, just a baby face.

"What should we call her?" Sloan asked, scooting her chair closer to the table to get a better look.

"How about baby Sally?" I shrugged. "It's better than just plain 'baby,' at least until we find out her real name."

"The bitch could have at least told us that much," Phyllis grumbled. "And what kind of stripper lets herself get pregnant."

"Maybe somebody slipped something in her drink," Gillian suggested seriously. It gave us all something to think about, and I didn't much like the thought.

If there were any truth in Gillian's suggestion, it would explain the stripper's unorthodox way of handling the situation. I had to admit that I would be furious, too, and determined to make somebody pay.

Then I shook my head. I couldn't believe I was actually starting to feel sorry for a woman who could leave a newborn baby in an empty house for someone to find, and entrust her to a group of women who were strangers. How did she know we wouldn't just take the baby to family services and drop her off? How did she know we would take care of her?

What the woman had done would be considered criminal. Then, maybe she was smart enough to realize that we wouldn't turn her in—not after we realized the baby belonged to one of our husbands.

Then I thought of something, something I couldn't believe none of us had even considered. "What if she's lying?" I blurted out. The baby had clasped her tiny fingers around my index finger. She has an amazingly strong grip, I thought, awed despite myself. I couldn't seem to take my eyes off baby Sally.

"For what purpose?" Phyllis asked.

"Yeah," Sloan said, her fascinated gaze glued to the baby as well. "Why would she lie?"

"For money?" I suggested. "You have to admit, we didn't even think about the possibility, which makes each and every one of us gullible fools."

"We're fooling ourselves," Gillian said, smashing my new theory. "We'd all like to think that this couldn't be happening, but it is. Baby Sally has a father, and he lives right here in the cove."

Gillian's bald words created an uneasy silence around the table. I felt sick to my stomach, because I knew that she was right. What had happened the night baby Sally was conceived? Had it been just a little harmless fun that got out of hand with a willing stripper—a professional? Or had something terrible, something darker happened that night?

The word gang rape came to my mind. I immediately pushed the horrible thought away. No. Not my Tracy. He couldn't or wouldn't harm a hair on anyone's head. First do no harm was one of the first things he learned in medical school.

But I knew, deep down inside, that Tracy being a doctor didn't make him any less human . . . or any less fallible.

"What are we going to do with baby Sally in the meantime?" Kara asked.

"I'll keep her," I said quickly.

"No, I'll keep her," Gillian said.

Sensing an argument, I made a suggestion. "Why don't we take

16

turns? Since she's already here, I'll keep her for a few nights. Then you can have her, Gillian." I was silently relieved when she didn't protest the arrangement. "In the meantime, let's find out all that we can about that night. Ask them. Badger them until they tell you. We'll meet back here tomorrow, same time."

"Gage won't be home until Monday," Gillian said.

"Call him," I suggested.

Phyllis stood. "Do we tell them about baby Sally?"

"If we do, they might panic and clam up," Natasha said sourly. "Especially Brandon, since he doesn't want kids."

She has a point, I thought. "Let's keep that information to ourselves for now, then. We can stick to the truth as much as possible, especially with the part about finding her in the Reed house. Since it's Friday, I'll tell Tracy that we have to wait until Monday before we can call social services."

Reluctantly, the others prepared to leave. Despite the circumstances, they each paused to look at baby Sally or reach out and touch her. It wasn't the baby's fault, no matter how things turned out, and I was glad that nobody seemed to blame her.

After they'd gone, I made a list of things baby Sally would need over the weekend, then checked her diaper to see how urgently I needed to get these supplies. Tracy was supposed to be home soon, but if it looked as if he wouldn't make it, I knew that I could send one of the other women.

Chapter 7

Time seemed to slow as I waited for Tracy. I played with baby Sally, even got a smile out of her, but I could tell she was growing hungry by the way she kept sucking on her fingers.

Finally, I heard Tracy's SUV in the drive. My heartbeat began to pick up as I heard him come in the front door. I tensed at the sound of his keys hitting the hall table, then heard his footsteps coming down the hall to the kitchen.

When he appeared in the doorway, my stomach bottomed out. I actually tasted bile, thinking about my husband, the man I loved with all my heart, committing adultery with baby Sally's mom. How could he if he loved me? And if it turned out that he had, what would I do about it?

"Honey?" He stopped when he saw me. Then his gaze dropped to the basket on the table and the baby inside. His brows rose. "Who's baby?"

If the situation hadn't been so serious, I might have laughed at the irony of his question.

Who's baby, indeed!

"Who's baby?"

As my husband asked the question, I gazed down at baby Sally lying in the basket. It was an odd feeling, knowing that I could be looking at a child my husband had fathered.

The feeling was odd because I was both appalled and strangely excited by the possibility.

"Honey?"

I jerked my gaze from the baby's face and licked my lips. "Someone left her inside the Reed house."

Tracy, understandably, looked blank. "What do you mean? You mean her mother left her? As in abandoned her?"

"Yeah, that's what I mean." Briefly, I recounted the afternoon's events leading up to the moment I brought her home with me. I naturally left out the part about the letter and its contents.

"You should call the police," Tracy advised, yanking on his tie and pulling it off. He draped it over a kitchen chair, staring at the baby as if he couldn't believe his eyes.

"What if something's wrong with her? If something bad happens while you have her, they could sue the hell out of you."

I hadn't thought of that. In any case, I knew things Tracy didn't know about baby Sally. Things he didn't know and things I wasn't ready to tell him.

"I'm not giving her to the police, Tracy. They probably wouldn't know what to do with her until Monday, when the children's services department can be called." I was fairly certain there was a hotline for situations like this, but maybe Tracy wasn't aware of it. He was a surgeon, not a pediatrician.

"And you know how to take care of her?" he asked, looking skeptical.

Stung by his tone, I said defensively, "I've baby-sat kids before. And I had two younger sisters, remember?" It was on the tip of my tongue to add that since he rarely saw my family, he might have forgotten. But I managed to swallow the words. The last thing I wanted was a fight. "I'm keeping her this weekend," I announced stubbornly, grabbing my purse. "And she needs some things from the store. Keep an eye on her until I get back."

"But—but—"

I ignored Tracy's sputtering and swept past him and out the door before he could find the words to protest. Since we didn't have a car seat for the baby, I couldn't take her with me. Besides, I thought, still miffed at Tracy for questioning my maternal instincts, maybe Tracy would see for himself that it didn't take a genius to watch over a tiny baby.

Chapter 8

Nevertheless, I hurried through my shopping, having second thoughts about leaving the baby with Tracy. Oh, I wasn't afraid he'd harm her, but I was beginning to fear that he'd ignore her. The thought of baby Sally crying her heart out made me floor the car on the way home. I careened around a curve and nearly lost control before I calmed down and drove sensibly.

I worried for nothing. The moment I walked into the house, I knew that everything had went fine. I knew because I could hear Tracy talking to baby Sally in this odd, gentle voice I'd never heard him use before.

"Now, now, pumpkin. I know you're hungry, but you'll just have to wait until Samantha gets back with your supper. I'm hungry, too, so I know how you feel."

The moment Tracy stopped talking, the baby began to whimper. I smiled as Tracy realized this and hastily began to speak to her again.

"There, there, precious. It will be all right. You just wait and see. We'll get you fixed up and before you know it, you'll have a full tummy."

My heart started to melt at his soft, consoling tone until I remembered why baby Sally was here in the first place. I straightened my shoulders, tightened my mouth, and barged into the kitchen. I pitched the bag of diapers to Tracy, who caught them instinctively.

"Here, you can change her while I mix her formula."

"But—but—"

"No, buts," I said briskly. "And while you're at it, check her out and make sure she's okay, doc."

"But, Samantha—"

"Tracy!" I turned to look at him. His panicked expression left me unmoved. This could be his child, after all. A child he had fathered with another woman. Why shouldn't he help? "Just help me, please."

"I've never changed a baby's diaper before," he blurted out, flushing when I lifted a derisive brow.

"There's a whole package of them to use for practice," I said, unrelenting. Poor Tracy, he had no idea why I was being so hard on him. Well, I wasn't ready to tell him, either, so he'd just have to keep on wondering for now. "If you want your supper, then you have to help me feed the baby her supper," I added a little more softly.

With a pained expression, Tracy gingerly lifted the baby and gathered her blanket out from under her. Then he spread the blanket on the table and ever so gently laid her down on the blanket. He studied the tabs on the disposable diaper a full moment before he gingerly pulled them open.

When I was certain he would figure it out without my help, I busied myself fixing the formula and boiling the new bottles I'd purchased.

Baby Sally was crying in earnest by the time I finally poured the warm formula into the sterilized bottle. I held the bottle out to Tracy. He shook his head and hastily handed the baby over to me.

"Maybe next time," he said. "I should get a shower before dinner."

Despite my angry mood, I bit back a smile at the rapid way he disappeared. I've never seen him move so fast, I thought, staring down at baby Sally's hungry face. She was gobbling the formula down as if she hadn't eaten in days.

When she'd finished the bottle, I burped her, then took her to our bedroom. I laid her down and moved our pillows so that she couldn't roll from the bed. For a long time, I stood there, just watching her. I found that I couldn't summon one shard of resentment toward the baby. If she turned out to belong to Tracy, then I would have to accept the fact.

I wasn't certain what I would do about Tracy, though, if he turned out to be the daddy. What a mess!

Back in the kitchen, I boiled some pasta and opened a jar of spaghetti sauce. Normally I enjoyed cooking, but tonight my mind wasn't on food. As I stirred the sauce, I tried to decide how to broach the subject of the bachelor party without arousing Tracy's suspicions about baby Sally.

Tracy's arms slid around me, startling a shriek from my lips. I tried to relax against him. "You scared me."

"Did I?" He nuzzled my neck, his breath warm against my skin. He smelled of soap and shampoo and deodorant.

Any other time I would have welcomed his caresses, but that was before baby Sally. Now I couldn't help wondering if he'd nuzzled the stripper the same way. My stomach lurched at the thought. I shivered.

"Cold?" Tracy asked, his hands moving lower.

I dropped the spoon and grabbed his hands before they reached ground zero. "I'm not in the mood, babe. It's . . . it's my PMS week." It was a lie, but I doubted that Tracy kept up with my menstrual cycle. At least, I hoped that he didn't.

Tracy shrugged and stepped back. I let out a silent sigh of relief and resumed stirring the sauce. Without turning around, I said, "Will you do the garlic bread? It's in the freezer."

"Sure. Anything for my sweet thang."

I forced a laugh at his customary teasing. "Did the baby seem okay to you?"

"Yeah, she seemed fine. I'm not a pediatrician, but she looked fit and healthy to me." He wrapped the garlic bread in foil and stuck it in the oven, then turned the knob. "I still think you should report this tonight, though."

"I don't want to."

He leaned against the counter next to me and folded his arms. I could feel him staring at me.

"You know that you can't keep this baby, Samantha. It doesn't work that way."

He had no idea how wrong he might possibly be. I fought the urge to cry. From the moment I met Tracy and fell in love with him, I'd struggled with the fear of losing him. My self-esteem—thanks to my stepmother and my distant father—had always been low. I just couldn't believe I was lucky enough to win the love of a man such as Tracy. Oh, it wasn't just that he came from a wealthy family, or that he was a doctor. I felt that he was way out of my league in every way. He was a special man, and I felt blessed.

When I told him my fears, he would laugh and tell me that he should be the one to count his blessings for finding me. Eventually, I was able to push my fears to the back of my mind.

Today, they were clamoring to get back out and make my life a living hell. I needed reassurance, and I was deathly afraid that I wouldn't get it. What if I couldn't give Tracy children? Would he end up dumping me for someone younger and capable of giving him a child, like Elliot Reed had dumped his wife?

Chapter 9

After dinner, I stacked our dishes in the dishwasher and put on some coffee. While the coffee was brewing, I asked Tracy to check on baby Sally.

He looked startled at the reminder. He'd obviously forgotten about our new houseguest.

"She's sleeping," he informed me when he returned. He looked angry and puzzled. "How could a mother do that to her baby?"

Tersely, I said, "How do you know it wasn't her daddy that abandoned her?"

Tracy didn't have an answer to that question, I realized after few moments. I poured our coffee and brought it to the table. This was something of a ritual for us—when Tracy did make it home—a time when we caught each other up on everything that had happened during the day. He told me about his patients and the surgeries, and I told him about birthday parties and the like.

"It was touch and go for a bit there, but we finally found the bleeder and clamped it off before we lost the patient," Tracy concluded, sighing as he leaned back in his chair. He looked exhausted, but that wasn't anything new. He was a dedicated surgeon and worked impossibly long hours.

When he wasn't attending bachelor parties and making out with strippers.

Fueled by this reminder, I took a deep breath and began my questioning. "Tracy, today the girls and I were talking about the bachelor party—"

"Not that again?" He groaned and rubbed his hands over his face. He shook his head. "Baby, we've been over this a dozen times. It's been a year, for goodness sake."

I was not to be derailed. "Even so, I don't think I can forget about it and put it behind us until you tell me the truth about what happened that night." Not surprisingly, Tracy immediately got that guarded expression I recognized anytime I mentioned the bachelor party. I'd lay odds the men had all decided to stick with the same story just to appease us.

Tracy was about to find out that I could match him any day in the stubborn department. I hoped the others were just as determined to get to the truth.

"It was just your ordinary bachelor party. Lot's of food, booze, and a girl jumping out of a cake. Kind of boring, really."

Boring? An image of the sleeping baby on our bed came to mind. Boring? I don't think so.

I pushed my coffee cup aside and laid the flat of my hands on the table. I stared at Tracy until he was forced to stare back. "I want you to start at the beginning. Tell me everything that you did that night, from the moment you got there, till the moment you left."

"Why?" Tracy asked, growing belligerent, like a little boy caught in the wrong but determined not to admit it. "It's over and done with. Why do we have to keep talking about it?"

Very softly and very seriously, I said, "Because our marriage is in jeopardy if you don't come clean with me."

Tracy raked his hand through his hair and hit the table with his fist. "Samantha, what's this about? Does it have anything to do with the mystery baby?"

Since I had been expecting something like this, I was able to keep my expression neutral. "It has nothing to do with her, but it has a lot to do with our future. If I'm going to share children with you and spend my life with you, I don't want any skeletons jumping out of the closet at a later date."

Tracy laughed at that. "I assure you, babe, that I don't have any illegitimate or legitimate children that I haven't told you about, if that's what you're implying. At least none that I know of," he added with a smile meant to soften me.

It didn't work because I didn't find it the least bit funny, but he couldn't have known why I didn't. I tried again. "Tracy, it happened over a year ago. Anything you did that night . . . well, it's already been done. I won't be mad." I wasn't being entirely truthful, but I felt justified.

"If it doesn't matter, then why do you have to know about it?"

Ah-ha! "So something did happen," I said, ignoring the sharp pain in my chest at the thought. "Tell me about it. I need to know."

"I got really drunk."

"Yes, so drunk you might have done something you might not otherwise have done if you were sober," I suggested cautiously.

Tracy looked away from my tense face. "Everything's really fuzzy about that night."

I didn't bother hiding my explosive, impatient sigh. "Tracy, you were obviously drunk, but you weren't that drunk. What happened at the party? Was the stripper the only woman there?" My stomach clenched in anticipation.

"No . . . yes, I mean, the bartender was a woman, but she stayed behind the bar." Tracy drummed his fingers on the bar and shot me an annoyed glance. "I told you how I got glitter in my pants. A couple of the guys did it, hoping you'd freak out."

"I want details, Tracy." My voice sounded hard and distant. I wished I felt hard and distance. Inside I was mush. "I want to know what happened after the stripper jumped from the cake. Until you tell me . . . there will be this lie between us, and it's driving me crazy."

"Dammit, Samantha!" Tracy's face was turning red, revealing his deep agitation. "What do you want to hear? That she had big tits? That she was a knockout, and could twist her body into positions none of us thought possible?" He leaned forward, angry enough now to look me in the eye. "When she stripped completely and started dancing on our laps, I wasn't the only one that forgot about the 'no touching' rule."

My mouth went dry. "What—what did you do?"

Tracy's gaze fell away. He sighed and threw back his head, staring at the ceiling. "I was so drunk, Samantha, and the guys . . . well, they were egging me on. We were all daring each other."

I could see it. In my mind's eye, I could see them all screaming in their macho men voices, daring each other. Egging each other on. The men were very competitive. I swallowed hard.

"Did—did the stripper mind you touching her?" My voice came out husky and faint, much to my disgust.

He shook his head. "Not really. In fact . . ." He hesitated, casting me a guilty glance. "In fact, I think she was hoping we would. I don't think she was there just to strip and dance, if you know what I mean."

"You think she was a prostitute?" I asked hoarsely.

He nodded. "Gage flashed a hundred dollar bill at her and told her to . . . um, unzip my pants and um, well—"

"Give you oral sex?" To my astonishment, my heart leaped with hope. Oral sex did not get people pregnant. Not that I didn't consider oral sex infidelity. It was in my book, although I suspected many men didn't think the same. "So that's how you got the glitter on your penis?"

"Yeah. She had the stuff all over her body." Tracy refused to look at me at all now.

"So you let her . . . ?" I felt sick just asking the questions, but I had to know.

Tracy stared at the floor. "Yeah, I think I did."

How could a man forget something so memorable? I didn't really believe that Tracy had forgotten, but I realized I had probably pushed him to his limit. But I had one more question that I had to ask him.

"Tracy, did you guys do any drugs that night?"

Startled, Tracy looked at me, and in that split second I saw the truth in his eyes. He couldn't lie to me now, although I figured he would try. To my surprise, he didn't.

He swung around in his chair and dropped his arms to his bent knees. "At the beginning of the party, we all did some Ecstacy. Ever heard of it?" When I nodded, he continued. "I still can't believe I did it, knowing what that stuff is made of and what it can do to your brain cells." He frowned. "Even Drew did it, and you know how paranoid he is about drugs."

"Where did this Ecstacy come from?"

He shot me a calculating look before he said, "Does it matter?"

I guess that it didn't, since they had all willingly taken it. Then I remembered what Sloan had said about Lee not remembering. "Was Lee aware that he was taking it?"

Tracy was silent for a long moment, as if he were trying to remember. Finally, he shrugged. "I can't answer that one. I think he knew it, but I couldn't swear on it."

To say I was shocked would be putting it mildly. We were not into drugs and never had been. As far as I knew, the other couples weren't either, with the exception of an occasional joint someone produced at an adult party.

I had one last very important question, and I braced myself for the answer. "Tracy, look at me." He did, but there was no mistaking the wary look in his eyes. "After the . . . oral sex, did you have any other physical contact with the stripper?"

"No."

I might have believed him if he'd kept on looking at me, but he didn't. His gaze slid from mine even as he spoke. He might have been embarrassed, or he might have been guilty.

"If you're through interrogating me, I think I'll watch the news before I turn in. I've got an early surgery tomorrow."

He was mad at me. Well, I was mad at him, too. With a sinking heart, I watched him leave the kitchen. What would this do to our marriage? It had already knocked a dent in my faith and trust in Tracy. Now, I knew that he was just as fallible as anyone. If he'd been unfaithful once, he could be unfaithful again. Did I want to live with this type of mistrust?

Tears slipped down my face. I felt as if someone was tearing me apart inside. I loved my husband. And I had been very happily married, or that's what I had believed.

Now I could no longer say I was.

Were my friends going through the same agony? And would we survive?

After a while, I wiped my face with a napkin and went to check on the baby. I found her awake and staring around our bedroom in wonder. Just watching her made the ache in my chest perversely stronger, yet easier. Whatever happened at that party, baby Sally was innocent.

I fed the baby, gave her a bath in the kitchen sink, then dressed her in a new sleeper I'd bought at the store. Using a laundry basket, I made her a bed and set it beside my bed. I was afraid to put her in bed with us, knowing that we might roll over and crush her.

By the time I put her down and crawled into bed, Tracy was fast asleep. I cried myself to sleep that night, frightened and worried about the future.

Who was baby Sally's daddy?

Around one in the morning, baby Sally awoke me with a hungry demand for another bottle. I gathered her up and stumbled into the kitchen so that we wouldn't wake Tracy. I laid her in the basket on the table as I heated the bottle, ruefully aware that when yearning for a baby, I hadn't quite thought about the endless feedings and sleepless nights I would have to endure.

As I yawned and rubbed my eyes and tried to stay awake, I wondered if I was cut out for motherhood. Yet, by the time baby Sally finished her bottle and drifted back to sleep, I was wide awake and feeling soft and maternal. It wasn't so bad, I decided.

I put baby Sally back to bed in her makeshift crib, then returned to the kitchen to rinse out the bottle. As I was rinsing it, I looked out the kitchen window, over to the Reed house next door. My breath caught sharply.

A light was in the house!

Heart pounding, I put the bottle aside, found my robe and slippers, and after checking on baby Sally one last time, I let myself out the front door.

Someone was at the Reed house, and I suspected it was baby Sally's mother. Who else could it be? With grim determination, I marched across our lawn onto the property next door. If she was in there, then I was going to have a talk with her. It was time to put an end to this cat and mouse game. I would find out for myself what happened at Lee's bachelor party!

My courage threatened to desert me at the front door. This was the Reed house, after all. A place where a grisly murder and suicide had taken place. A house that gave me the creeps.

The door was slightly ajar, and as I gathered my nerve and pushed it further open, I heard the sound of someone crying. It wasn't a loud sound, but it was recognizable.

I crept inside, hesitating. I have to admit that I came very close to turning around and running back out that door.

Only the image of baby Sally, fast asleep in my laundry basket at home, stopped me. Someone was playing a cruel game with her life, and ours, and I wanted to get to the bottom of it.

So I forced my trembling legs to continue. I moved from the foyer into the living area, following the sound and the light, wishing the entire house was lit so that my heart wouldn't beat quite so hard inside my chest.

The sound appeared to be coming from another room beyond the living room. I'd never been in the house before that day, so I didn't know the layout. I had to move slowly, although I knew there wasn't any danger of me bumping into furniture; the house was empty.

Finally, I came to the doorway of the room where the flickering light was shining.

Standing by an empty fireplace was a tall, blond woman. She had her head bent, crying into her hands, so I couldn't see her face. The light came from a candle on the fireplace mantel.

The sounds she was making seemed to be torn from her very soul. This woman was in pain. Not the physical kind, I suspected, but the mental kind.

And despite my anger, I felt a stirring of pity.

"Hello?" I said softly.

The crying stopped abruptly. I heard her suck in a little gasp. She dropped her hands and swung around to stare at me for a second, her expression one of acute dismay.

Then she ran, cutting through a doorway at the opposite end of the room. Without thinking, I took out after her. She wore shoes as opposed to my house slippers, so I could follow her footsteps with ease.

But she was faster than me, and before I could catch up with her, she crashed through the back door and disappeared into the night.

I stopped, my breath rasping in my throat. I tried to think. Where would she go? She couldn't have been on foot, could she? The realization gave me an idea.

I reversed directions and headed back through the house to the front door. Just as I stumbled onto the front porch, I heard the sound of a car screeching away. As I watched it disappear, I let out a frustrated curse.

It appeared I wouldn't be getting anything settled tonight, as I'd hoped when I realized who the intruder must be. What was she doing here, at the Reed house? Why had she left her baby? Why had she come back and risk someone seeing her? Was this part of the game she was playing?

Chapter 10

Reluctantly, I retraced my steps and picked up the burning candle from the mantel. I was alone in Reed house.

The realization struck me hard. My hands began to shake, making the candlelight dance eerily upon the walls. Steeling myself, I started to carry the candle from the house.

My foot bumped against something on the floor. Stifling a frightened shriek, I bent down and retrieved the object.

It was a fashion magazine, faded and mangled, as if it had been clutched in someone's sweaty hands and constantly looked at.

On the cover, there was a blonde model; her crystal blue eyes smiling along with her perfectly painted mouth. A gold tunic draped from one slender, smooth shoulder, revealing a hint of cleavage.

It wasn't the face of the woman I'd just seen, though. The model looked older, wiser.

The date on the magazine showed that it was four years old. So? It could have been left in the house, overlooked by the Realtors, I told myself.

I didn't believe it for a moment.

Our mystery woman/mother had brought the magazine with her, and had left it behind when I startled her into flight.

I gripped the magazine and the candle and hurried from the house, letting out a relieved sigh when I made it to the porch. I locked and closed the front door, wondering how the woman was getting inside. She must have a key. Either that, or she was a talented burglar with the right tools.

Whatever her talents . . . and I remembered, then, with a sickening lurch of my stomach, that she had many according to Tracy, she was apparently going through a breakdown of some type.

Clutching the magazine and the candle, I froze on the porch of Reed house. Our mystery woman hadn't seemed like a woman playing games.

She had been crying as if she were remembering a tragedy.

The expression, "gang rape" crept into my mind again, horrifying me with its implications. Could it be true? Had our husbands, reckless with drink and fueled by the libido-enhancing drug Ecstasy, taken advantage of the stripper that night?

In another time and place—before yesterday—I would have been the first to laugh at such a possibility. Tracy was a doctor. He saved lives. The thought of him committing a horrible crime like rape would never have crossed my mind in a million years.

But it was becoming more and more apparent that something bad had happened the night of Lee's bachelor party.

"We were daring each other," Tracy had told me. Could that dare have gotten out of hand? Could it have progressed into something more sinister? And if it had, why hadn't the woman gone to the police afterward?

I supposed it was possible that she feared the police wouldn't have believed her. She was, after all, a professional stripper, and, according to Tracy, a woman who could be bought.

Chapter 11

Once back in my own house, I put the magazine away in a kitchen drawer. When I met with the others later, I would show them the magazine. Maybe someone would recognize the model and shed some light on the finding. If the magazine held any significance at all.

I briefly considered alerting the agency about the woman at Reed house, but decided against it. I wanted her to come back. Perhaps the next time I could convince her to talk to me.

Baby Sally demanded another feeding at four o'clock. This time it was Tracy who heard her cries. He shook me gently.

"Honey, the baby's crying. I thought I was dreaming."

Exhausted from baby Sally's earlier feeding and my subsequent early-hour detective work, I moaned and buried my head in the pillow. My voice was muffled as I said, "Why don't you feed her this time?"

"Hey, I'm not the one who brought her home and insisted on keeping her till Monday." Tracy slapped me on the bottom. "Besides, I've got surgery at six, so I've got to get going."

I silently cursed him when I heard the sound of the shower. Rolling over in bed, I peered over the edge at the baby. I couldn't help but smile.

She was furious, her little face scrunched and red. She flayed her fists around as if seeking someone to punch for this outrage. Chuckling, I gathered her up and took her into the kitchen.

"Coffee first, Sally," I said as I settled her into the basket. "Or you might get fruit-flavored punch instead of milk." The moment I let go, she began to howl. Hastily, I got the coffeemaker going and heated her a bottle. While the bottle was heating, I changed her diaper and checked her sleeper.

Baby Sally screamed the entire time.

"Okay, okay," I admonished her gently. "I get the picture." I cradled her in my arms, tested the bottle again, and gave it to her. She sucked hungrily, making smacking noises and grabbing at the bottle with her tiny little hands.

Holding her tiny body while she drank her breakfast gave me a warm feeling all over. She wasn't my baby, true, but she was a baby, and in my opinion, all babies were magic. I'd seen them turn the most determined, hardened cynic into a blubbering, baby-talking fool. I was no exception, and neither was Tracy.

The rest of the day, I stayed so busy with baby Sally that I wasn't aware of the time passing until Phyllis came in. She took one look at my exhausted, flushed face and took the baby.

"Good grief, Samantha. You look like you've been rode hard and hung up wet."

I couldn't help smiling at her old western cliche. "I feel like it, too," I confessed.

Phyllis had been holding the baby all of five minutes when Kara arrived and took her. Those two were fighting over the baby when Gillian, Natasha, and Sloan arrived.

Sloan looked as if she'd cried all night. Her eyes were swollen and her face was blotched and red.

Ruthlessly, I took the sleeping baby from Kara and put her down in her makeshift bed so that she could finish her nap in peace.

"Hey, why did you do that? I could have held her," Kara protested when I returned from putting baby Sally to bed.

"We need to talk," I reminded her. I stood with my hands on my hips, staring at the mound of items each of them had piled on the kitchen counter when they came in. Toys, more diapers, sleepers, T-shirts, and to my amazement, a car seat with the price tag still attached.

It appeared that I wasn't the only one crazy. How, I wondered, can we be so accepting of this baby when she could likely ruin our lives? I think it said a lot for the gentle, loving characters of each woman of Reed Cove.

If the stripper decided to leave her child with its natural father— once we figured out who it was—then I knew that baby Sally would have a good home. Maybe the relief I felt knowing this was misplaced, but I felt it just the same.

As they all took their places at the table, I opened a kitchen drawer and took out the magazine. I set it in the middle of the table and told them about finding the woman crying in Reed house, and about finding the magazine. "Anyone recognize this woman?"

Five pairs of eyes focused on the blonde cover model.

And I saw recognition on every single face.

It was Phyllis who delivered the bombshell, and she did it in a voice hoarse with disbelief. "It can't be her! Baby Sally's mother can not be Kelly Reed! Kelly Reed is dead. I went to her funeral, I saw her in the casket. Her husband shot her in the—"

I interrupted her babbling, tapping the magazine. "Phylicia, calm down. This isn't the same woman I saw early this morning, although the resemblance is uncanny." I took a deep breath as a possibility occurred to me. "Did Kelly have a sister?"

Gillian spoke up, looking dazed. "Yeah, she did, but she was much younger than Kelly. In fact, she was still in high school at the time of Kelly's death."

I unglued my tongue from the roof of my mouth. "The woman I saw this morning was young. Very young."

"Her name was Amber," Natasha said slowly. "I saw her once or twice when she came to visit Kelly." She shook her head and let out a long breath. "I can't believe I didn't recognize her yesterday."

"So the woman you saw yesterday was Amber?" I asked, feeling a fluttering of excitement. I felt that we were finally getting somewhere.

"Yes, that was her."

"What does it all mean?" Sloan wanted to know. She was wringing her hands and looked on the verge of tears again. "Lee admitted that he let her perform oral sex on him, but he swears he never touched her afterward."

"Gage said the same thing!"

"That's what Luke said, too."

"Same here," Phyllis inserted tightly. She looked at me and I nodded. She muttered a nasty oath. "Obviously, someone is lying."

"Maybe they all are," I blurted out. "Maybe it was a gang rape by our husbands. Tracy admitted they'd all taken Ecstacy, which I've heard enhances the libido."

"Makes them horny," Phyllis translated furiously. "God, this is such a mess!"

Sloan burst into noisy sobs. I went to her and put my hands on her shoulders. "We'll get to the bottom of this, Sloan. I promise."

Through her sobs, Sloan voiced a concern that I think was on all our minds. "That's—that's what I'm afraid of! What if—if Lee's the father of baby Sally? I don't know if I can—can stay married to him, knowing he slept with someone else."

What would I do if it turned out to be Tracy?

"Well," Natasha said in miserable voice. "I guess there's only one thing left for us to do."

We all looked at her expectantly.

"We'll have to make them take a blood test. That should narrow it down. Then, if one of them doesn't confess, we'll have to get them to agree to a DNA test."

"If they won't confess," Phyllis pointed out, "how can we force them to participate in a DNA test?"

I knew the answer to that one. "They wouldn't have to know about it until afterward." It might be underhanded, but I knew that I would do it if I had to.

One of them was the daddy, and I intended to find out.

Sloan Kelly, Reed's sister, Amber, was baby Sally Jane's mother. It seemed to be the only thing we all agreed upon.

If only Natasha's husband, Brandon, hadn't hired Amber, the

33

stripper, for Lee's bachelor party. If only they hadn't gotten so drunk. If only they hadn't taken the drug Ecstacy.

There were a lot of "if onlys" going through my mind, and I suspected I wasn't the only one. But wishing wouldn't change the facts. Someone had gotten the stripper pregnant the night of the bachelor party.

The meeting dragged on and on, and several times I had to break up an argument. Everyone was on edge, of course. How could we not be, each of us thinking our husband was baby Sally Jane's father?

Finally, after what felt like hours, we came to an agreement on how we planned to tell the men about baby Sally Jane. It was Phylicia's idea, originally.

"Getting them all together is the best way," Phyllis said. "They won't be as likely to try and place the blame on each other, if they're face to face."

I nodded. "I think Phylicia's right. It's not only time-consuming doing it separately, I don't think it's as effective."

"They'll be furious with us," Sloan whispered.

"So?" Natasha snarled. "As if we aren't already furious with them? I don't know about the rest of you, but in my book oral sex is adultery."

We all agreed. I think that deep down some of us would like to think that allowing a woman to perform oral sex wasn't the same thing as intercourse, but nobody was willing to admit this aloud.

"Let's plan a get together in the park tomorrow," I suggested, ready for the meeting to be over with. I was getting a headache. "A picnic. Sunday is the only day when all the men might be home."

"What if they aren't? What if one of them can't make it? It wouldn't be fair."

Kara had a good point.

"Well, we'll just have to use our persuasive talents to make sure they are there." I looked at each pensive face, wondering if we'd all make it out of this mess and still be friends. One thing seemed certain; five of us would be relieved, and one of us would be devastated. Shamelessly, I hoped it wouldn't be me.

"We should get baby-sitters for the kids," Gillian said. "With the exception of baby Sally Jane. I think she should be there."

Thankfully, the picnic was arranged for two o'clock, and the ladies left me alone with my own insecurities and a baby who held a great deal of power over our futures. Gillian seemed to have forgotten that she had wanted to keep the baby. I couldn't help but wonder if her oversight had been deliberate.

It wasn't baby Sally Jane's fault, I knew, but I had no control over how the other's felt about the baby.

I spent another night getting up and down with baby Sally Jane, who seemed to be hungry a lot, which made me wonder if her mother had been feeding her cereal or baby food. How was I to know? When I thought about it too much, I became furious all over again at the way Sally Jane's mother had just left her with strangers. How did she know there wasn't a psycho among us? How did she know one of us wouldn't kill baby Sally Jane and bury her where nobody would ever find her? Where would her evidence be then? How would she play her devious game without baby Sally Jane?

Foolish thoughts, but then, you have to remember that I was exhausted. I would never hurt baby Sally Jane.

Each time I got up with Sally Jane, I looked out the window over to the Reed house, but I never saw another light. Near dawn, I gave up and settled in for a few hours sleep. Tracy had called around midnight saying he had an emergency surgery and probably wouldn't be home until the morning hours. I didn't tell him about the picnic, deciding to wait until he got home.

Chapter 12

It was seven o'clock when I got the call. I'd been lying in bed, dozing off and on and waiting for Sally Jane to wake up for her morning feeding when the phone rang.

Groggily, I reached over and picked up the receiver, thinking it would be Tracy telling me he was on his way home. He often called first to see if he needed to pick up anything for me on the way. In fact, I was so certain that it would be Tracy that I didn't bother saying hello.

"So, you're on your way home?"

"Hello?" a strange voice queried, making me feel foolish.

"Oh, I thought you were my husband. I'm sorry."

"Is Ally okay?"

"Excuse me? I think you have the wrong—"

"The baby. My baby. Her name is Allyson."

I was floored into temporary silence. Finally, I found my tongue. "Is this Amber?"

There was a stunned pause, then, "So you figured out who I am, Samantha. Have you figured out who Ally's daddy is?"

"Don't you know?" I asked waspishly.

"If I did, you wouldn't be taking care of her right now," she replied cryptically. "And you can can the hostility. I wasn't alone when Ally was conceived."

My blood began to boil. "No, you weren't. You were having unprotected sex with six married men." An awful idea suddenly struck me. What if she had AIDS or some other sexually transmitted disease? How could Tracy have been so damned careless? Not only with his own life, but with mine?

"It wasn't like that," Amber said, her voice strangely thick. "Haven't you asked them about that night?"

"Yeah. They all admit to getting a blow job from yours truly." When she didn't immediately reply, I felt a jolt of vicious satisfaction. Hopefully, I had wounded her. She had it coming, as far as I was concerned. And I wasn't finished. "What do you want, money?"

"No, I don't want your money. I want justice."

She hung up, leaving me to mull over her mysterious statement. She wanted justice. What did that mean? Another, more chilling thought occurred to me.

She had known my name, and my phone number. She knew I was keeping baby Sally Jane—no, it was Ally. The baby's name was

Allyson. I had to remember that.

Was she stalking me? To know the things she knew, she had to be watching the house. Goose bumps flared on my arms at the thought. Maybe I should call the police after all. Maybe Amber was a psycho.

But I cringed at telling the police the whole sordid story, which could wind up in the newspapers. No, I wouldn't go that route yet. So what if she knew I was taking care of her baby? She hadn't said anything threatening, other than saying that she wanted justice. I assumed she was talking about someone taking responsibility for getting her pregnant.

The ringing phone had awakened the baby, so I got up and took her into the kitchen to heat her a bottle. Funny, how it felt as if I had been doing this kind of thing for more than two days. I guess all it took was a little practice to get the hang of it.

Chapter 13

A million questions ran through my mind as I fed Ally. Did Amber miss her baby? What had she meant by wanting justice? Why didn't she just tell me?

Phyllis came in as I was changing the baby. "I haven't slept a wink all night," she said irritably. Without glancing at the baby, she poured herself a cup of coffee and went to stand by the back door. She opened it a crack and inhaled deeply. "How about you?"

"Not much," I said as I gently worked Ally's arms through the sleeves of a clean T-shirt. It was warm in the house, so I left her with a diaper and the T-shirt. I moved her into the living room—away from the smoke—and put her on a blanket in the floor, positioning her so that I could still see her from the kitchen. She immediately began pumping her legs and arms, squealing with delight.

Back in the kitchen, I poured another cup of coffee and sat down at the table. Phyllis joined me. Our gazes met. "I got a call from Amber this morning. She said she wanted justice."

"What?"

I nodded. "That's what she said. Doesn't make sense. I asked her if she was after money, and that's when she said she wanted justice." When Phyllis flushed and looked away, I narrowed my eyes on her. "Phylicia? Is there something you need to tell me? Do you know what she meant by 'justice?'"

"I don't know. Maybe. It's probably a long shot, but—"

"Tell me," I demanded, trying to control my impulse to reach out and slap her. If she knew something and wasn't telling, I knew that I wouldn't be the only one furious.

"Well, it's about Sloan Kelly."

I shook my head, completely confused. "Sloan Kelly's dead. How can this be about her?"

"Because Sloan Kelly's Amber's sister." It was obvious that Phyllis was very nervous. "Sloan Kelly and Amber were close. In fact, Sloan Kelly was basically supporting her mother and Amber, and planned on putting Amber through college." She glanced briefly at me. "At least this is what Sloan Kelly told me."

"You and Sloan Kelly were friends? I thought nobody liked her."

Phyllis shrugged. "She wasn't that bad. A little vain. She was a schemer, too. She actually told me that she married Allen for his money, and lied about wanting kids."

Very softly, I asked, "And you told Allen? Is that why Sloan Kelly's doing this?"

"No! No, I didn't tell Allen. I would never do that." Then, almost in a whisper, she added, "But I told Drew."

"And Drew told Allen."

She nodded. Her bottom lip trembled, and tears hovered in her bloodshot eyes. "I never dreamed he would tell Allen." A fat tear slipped over her bottom lashes and trekked down her cheek. She licked it away, staring at the table. "I doubt that Drew had any idea Allen would take it so hard, you know? I mean, Drew felt awful about it, and nearly drove himself crazy with guilt."

I was dazed by her confession. "So . . . because of what Drew told him, Allen shot Sloan Kelly, then killed himself?"

"Yeah, I guess. I mean, why else would Allen shoot his wife and kill himself?"

She had a point, not that I agreed that the tragedy was Drew's fault. He wasn't responsible for Allen's heinous actions. Drew hadn't forced Allen to pull the trigger.

I frowned down at my coffee, trying to put the pieces of the puzzle together. "Now I can understand why Amber might want to hurt Drew . . . and even you, if she knows, but what about the rest of us?"

Phyllis didn't have an answer. "I don't know, Samantha. That's why I haven't said anything. I didn't connect the dots until we found out that Amber was the stripper at the party. Then I started thinking and remembering. I'd almost forgotten about it, you know. It's not something I wanted to remember, so I just pushed it from my mind."

I could certainly understand why. Slowly, I put words to my thoughts, hoping Phyllis would help me figure it out. "So when Amber found out that Drew was going to be at the party, she decided to get a little revenge, maybe?"

"Maybe."

"But somehow, it backfired on her, and now she wants justice."

"Possibly. When we talked to the guys . . . maybe they'll tell us what happened, and we can put the rest of the pieces of this puzzle together."

"You know that we'll have to tell the others about this. It would only be fair."

Phyllis folded her arms, her chest hitching on a sob. "I know, I know. Dammit! Why did this have to happen to us?"

Unfortunately, I didn't have an answer.

Chapter 14

At the picnic, we managed to get rid of two of the men by sending them after ice and beer. The other four stood around laughing and joking, totally unaware of the bombshell we were about to drop.

When everyone—meaning the women—was gathered around the picnic tables setting out food, Phyllis quickly and quietly told them what she'd told me. Before anyone could question her, the other men came back.

Finally, after everyone had eaten—those of us who could eat—I nervously stood up and captured everyone's attention by clapping my hands.

"Here, here!" Drew cried, creating laughter among the men. Their laughter faded when they realized none of the women were smiling.

Swallowing a lump, I picked Ally up from the car seat and held her in front of me, facing the men. "What I'm about to tell you all will be a shock, but please don't ask questions until I'm finished."

Tracy, however, wasn't listening. "Honey, what are you doing? Holding an auction? Didn't I tell you that you couldn't keep the baby?" He looked at Drew, the lawyer. "Tell her, Drew. I'm afraid she's getting attached to the orphan—"

"She's not an orphan," I broke in coldly. "She belongs to a stripper named Amber. Sound familiar?" I could see by their suddenly still faces that it did. Tracy took a step in my direction, but I stopped him cold. "No, Tracy. Just listen. This is serious." He stopped and shoved his hands in his pockets, his expression grim.

He was angry, but I couldn't let that stop me. We had to know before one of us—or all of us—had to be carted off to the loony bin.

Everyone had fallen deathly silent. Even the birds had stopped chirping. My mouth felt like a desert as I continued. "Amber left this baby in the Reed house with a note, claiming that the baby was conceived the night of the bachelor party." I saw more than one guilty face before they concealed their expressions.

One of them was Tracy.

Fighting sudden nausea, I said, "So now do you understand why we have to know what happened that night? We pretty much know that Drew slept with her—"

"Hey!" Drew protested furiously, "How would you know that?"

Phyllis answered. "Because Amber is Sloan Kelly's sister. She was out for revenge. I'm sure she was planning on telling me all the

40

juicy details." Phyllis broke down and started crying, but when Drew tried to go to her, she held up her hand to ward him off. "No, don't! Don't you know why she wants revenge, Drew? Remember how you thought you were doing the right thing by telling Allen about Sloan Kelly getting an abortion?"

The color drained from Drew's face. Clearly, he remembered. "That bitch," he whispered in a choked voice. "That stripper bitch set me up!"

"I think it backfired," I said, indicating Ally in my arms. "I don't think she counted on getting pregnant." I paused deliberately before I added, "Or gang raped."

Several shocked gasps followed my statement, all from the men. The women looked at their husbands with red-rimmed, accusing eyes.

My gaze met Tracy's. Inside, I was a jittery mass of nerves. "Will you be first, Tracy? Will you tell us what you did that night?"

Tracy's chin jutted forward. "I've already told you what happened. I don't have anything to add."

I felt as if my heart was breaking. "And that's your final word?" Tracy's Adam's apple bobbed up and down, a tell-tale sign of his nervousness.

"Yes."

One by one, the others said basically the same thing, with the exception of Drew. He was glaringly silent. Obviously guilty.

And furious, as it turns out.

Red-faced, he swung to face the other men. "I'm not taking this rap for you guys," he spat out. "Tell them the truth, or I will."

I think my heart stood still as we all waited to see how the others would react to Drew's threat.

Lee was the first to speak. "She—she let him, so I thought—well, I thought—"

"That you might as well be next?" Sloan finished for him.

For a woman who had cried almost nonstop since finding the baby, she was amazingly calm now. The eye of the storm, I thought to myself.

Lee's face crumpled. "Honey, she didn't mean anything, I swear! I was so drunk, and that damned Ecstacy—"

"She passed out after I . . . finished," Drew inserted tautly.

I actually had to hold my hand over my mouth to keep from shrieking. Somehow, I managed to talk. "You—she wasn't even conscious?" I asked, my voice shrill. "You all had sex with an unconscious woman?"

Not a single one would look me in the eye. Ally cooed and jabbered, completely unaware of the tension in the air.

Now I knew why Amber wanted justice. Despite her own

41

underhanded attempts at revenge, what they had done was wrong. What they had done amounted to gang rape, something that had occurred to me in one of my darkest moments, but not something I had really believed could happen to us. Oh, God!

I stumbled to the picnic bench and sat down before my legs folded beneath me. With shaking arms, I transferred Ally back to the car seat.

Then I put my head onto my arms and cried.

"Honey?"

Chapter 15

It was Tracy, sounding agonized, guilty, and frightened all at once. Understandably, I couldn't muster any sympathy for him. I couldn't muster much sympathy for Amber, either, because what happened to her might not have happened at all if she hadn't been intent on getting revenge for her sister's death.

But her plan had backfired. Oh, yeah, it had backfired a lot. Badly. It had become a nightmare, in fact.

Yet . . . as I lifted my tear-soaked face and looked at the baby, I realized that I wasn't being entirely truthful.

Ally wasn't a nightmare. She was a miracle. A gift from God. A baby, fathered by Tracy, Drew, Lee, Luke, Gage, or Brandon. If Amber was a cat, then she might have had a kitten fathered by each one. Cats could do that, or so I'm told.

And then Drew dropped another bomb.

"She made me use a condom. I can't be the father."

When I started laughing—hysterically, of course—I was amazed when nobody joined me. Was I the only one that saw the irony in what Drew said—if he could be believed?

I finally got myself under control and wiped my eyes, staring at him in complete disbelief. "You don't mind if we insist on a blood test anyway, do you?" I asked sarcastically.

A muscle worked in his jaw. "No," he said through gritted teeth, as if I were the bad guy. "Go right ahead."

After the weekend I had had, I was grateful when Gillian volunteered to take Ally for the night. I was a little reluctant, though, and Gillian sensed it.

"I'm not going to smother her in her sleep," she said with a forced smile. "Believe me, if anyone's in danger it would be Gage, just because he's male."

"I know." I knew my face was red, but Gillian didn't seem to take offense at my hesitation. In fact, she reached out and hugged me, whispering in my ear.

"It will turn out okay, you'll see."

But how could it? Ally had a daddy, and it had to be one of the six men living in our cove.

After we got home, Tracy tried to talk to me. I wasn't in the mood to hear more lies, though.

"Samantha, we need to work this out."

I looked at him, frightened to discover I felt nothing. Maybe I

43

was numb. "How many other women have you slept with that I don't know about?" I asked.

He shook his head. "None. I swear."

"Yeah, right. And you swore you didn't sleep with Amber, either. Then you admitted that you did. I'm supposed to believe you now?"

"Having . . . sex with Amber was different than having an affair. I was drunk and high on Ecstacy. It was a bachelor party," he added, as if that made all the difference in the world.

"Oh," I said, blinking. "How stupid of me. Those excuses make everything all better. I think I'll go take a nap." I turned, then swung back around, my voice cold and emotionless, like I felt inside. "By the way, you can sleep on the couch for the time being."

"Honey—"

"No, Tracy, not yet. I can't forgive you yet. Maybe not ever."

He sounded desperate as he said, "We'll see a marriage counselor."

"Yeah, we probably will, but I don't know if it will help."

I knew I was being hard on him, but at the time I couldn't be any other way. My husband had not only committed adultery, he'd taken advantage of an unconscious woman and possibly fathered a child by her.

Chapter 16

The following day, the men took turns giving blood at a private clinic. They refused to have it done at the hospital where Tracy worked, claiming he could easily tamper with the results.

Sadly, I agreed with them. I no longer trusted my husband. We all no longer trusted each other. That's what this baby had done to each of us. It made us not trust our husbands or each other.

Ally also gave blood, and we got the count down from six to three possibilities.

I wished I could say that Tracy wasn't one of them and that we lived happily ever after.

But I can't, because Tracy was one of them.

And so was Drew. So much for his claim that he'd used a condom.

Lee was the third possible match, and Sloan promptly kicked him out of the house and called a lawyer.

After much debate, the men reluctantly agreed to a DNA test, which we all knew could take a few weeks. In the meantime, Gillian, Kara, and myself alternated the baby.

Despite it all, I was becoming very attached to Ally. Sometimes I found myself speculating on how I would react if Ally did belong to Tracy. Would it be so terrible? After all, Tracy had already confessed his biggest sin. Ally might be a result of that sin, but she was innocent.

Could I forgive him? Could I accept Ally if she turned out to belong to Tracy?

Yes, I thought I could. But I wasn't sure about forgiving Tracy. That was still up in the air, and it had nothing to do with whether he turned out to be the father.

About a week after the DNA tests, I was up in the wee hours of the morning feeding Ally when I noticed a flash of light in the Reed house. It was a habit now to look out the window whenever I walked past it at night.

I froze, thinking I might have imagined it. Then I saw it again. Yes, there was someone there. And I knew who that someone was.

With grim determination, I marched Ally into the living room and plopped her down beside Tracy, who was still sleeping on the couch. I shook him awake. "Watch the baby. I'm going to talk to Amber."

"She's here?" he asked, rubbing sleep from his eyes.

"No, she's at Reed house, I think."

"Be careful."

Somewhere along the way, I'd lost my fear of Reed house, I realized as I tiptoed through the dew-wet grass to the front door.

This time, it was closed and locked.

Undeterred, I rang the doorbell over and over. On the other side of the door, I heard footsteps.

"I know you're in there, Amber!" I shouted, not caring who heard me. "We need to talk, so let me in."

After what seemed like an eternity, the door opened and Amber stood there, holding a flash light. She was several inches taller than me, and I wasn't a short person. With her blond hair, leggy figure, and blue eyes, I could imagine how successful she was as a stripper.

"Come on in," she said, waving the light.

I stepped inside and faced her, getting right to the point. "They told us what they did to you. We also know what you were trying to do to Drew and Phylicia."

Amber had been crying. Her mascara was smeared under her eyes, and they were puffy and red-rimmed. "It wasn't anything compared to what they did to my sister," she said harshly. "They're the reason she's dead."

"No," I countered, "Allen's the reason she's dead. He pulled the trigger, not Drew or Phylicia. They couldn't have known Allen would go crazy."

"They should have kept their mouths shut!"

"And your sister should have been honest with her husband!" I shot back just as angrily. "If she hadn't been a lying, conniving bitch, then none of this would have happened."

Amber slapped me hard. My neck snapped back, but I didn't waver in my stance. I suppose I deserved it, talking about a dead woman that way, but all the stress I'd been under had turned me into a woman on the edge.

"You didn't even know my sister!" Amber hissed.

"No, I didn't," I admitted. "But everyone else in the cove did, and they all have the same opinion of her. I know these women, and they wouldn't lie about something like that."

The fight went out of Amber suddenly. It took me a moment to realize that she was crying again.

"She might have been a bitch, but she was good to me," she sobbed out. "She—she took care of me and Mom, and she was going to send me to college. Mom had a heart attack when she heard about Sloan Kelly's death." She wiped roughly at her face, as if she was ashamed to cry in front of me. But it did no good; the tears kept coming fast and furiously. "I had to quit school and get a job, then Mom died . . . and I had nobody. I had—had to get a different job just so I could pay the rent on my apartment."

For the first time in a week, I felt something besides anger or bitterness. I actually felt sympathy for this woman. Maybe it was misplaced—in light of the hell she'd put us all through—but it was there.

Tentatively, I reached out and put my hand on her shoulder in a comforting gesture. "Amber, Drew and Phyllis feel awful about what happened to Sloan Kelly. Phyllis said that Drew nearly had a nervous breakdown over it. But you've got to understand that it wasn't their fault your sister died. Allen was obviously unbalanced. Sane people don't go around shooting people and then themselves."

Sobbing now, Amber fell against the door and slid to the floor. I stood there, watching her cry and wishing I could do something. After hearing her story, I could understand how she could have blamed Drew and Phyllis for her sister's death. She'd hadn't been much more than a child herself at the time.

Finally, when she'd cried herself out, I knelt down next to her. "Do you want to come see Ally?"

Her eyes lit up at the mention of her baby. "Yeah, I do! I miss her so much!"

Together, we walked to my house. I took Ally from my sleeping husband's arms and brought her to Amber, who waited in the kitchen. As I watched the happy reunion, I began to cry uncontrollably. This was insane, I thought. Right in my kitchen, the stripper who slept with my husband was holding a baby that could belong to him.

Tracy woke up and came into the kitchen. When he saw Amber, his face went from white to red in a matter of seconds. He put his arms around me. "What are you doing here?" he asked Amber.

Amber's chin came out defiantly. At that moment she looked very young and vulnerable, and I felt ashamed for what the men had done to her.

"I'm here to see my baby. I'm gonna take her home."

"Leave her alone, Tracy," I croaked, pushing him away. "I think you've done enough damage."

To Amber, I said, "We should have the results from the DNA tests by the first of next week. Whoever the father is, he's going to take full responsibility for Ally."

"I could use some help," Amber admitted, her gaze on the sleeping baby in her arms. "But you shouldn't be so mad at your husband. I guess it was my fault they—they got so rowdy."

"Come again?" I held my breath, waiting for her answer.

She shrugged, and kept her gaze on the baby. I could see a guilty flush rising from her neck. She was quite pale, so it was easy to see. "I gave them a double-dose of Ecstacy. I wanted Drew to take it so that I could seduce him, but he wouldn't unless the others did."

My hands clenched. I had to bite down hard on my tongue to keep from racing at her and shrieking curses. I also had to remind myself several times that she'd suffered, and that her role model had been a conniving, selfish gold digger. And she was young, very young.

So I managed to keep my mouth shut and my hands to myself. Barely. With admirable calm, I gathered Ally's things; things the "snots" of Reed Cove had bought her. "Leave me your number," I said, struggling for civility. "And we'll get in touch with you."

"Okay." Amber sniffed, hugging her baby close. Her light blue eyes focused on my face. She must have seen a hint of my carefully controlled rage. "I'm sorry, Samantha. I didn't mean for things to turn out this way."

I believed her. But I knew that she had intended to ruin Phyllis and Drew's marriage. I swallowed hard and said, "No, I'm sure you didn't."

"But I can't say I'm sorry for having Ally." She took the pen that Tracy gave her and scribbled her number on a piece of paper he'd torn from the morning newspaper.

Once that was done, I led her to the front door, desperate to get her out of my house before I lost my temper in front of Ally. I looped the bulging diaper bag over her shoulder and kissed Ally on the forehead. She really is a sweet baby, I thought with a pang of yearning. Maybe someday Tracy and I would have a baby.

The thought brought me up short. So was I, then, considering staying with Tracy and trying to glue our marriage back together? If he hadn't taken the drugs, would he have slept with Amber anyway? I don't know if I would ever have satisfying answers to these questions.

Chapter 17

The next day I told the others about Amber's confession concerning the drugs she'd coaxed them into taking. They all looked relieved.

I knew how they felt. I had just made it easier for them to forgive and forget, if they could.

Tracy and I sat down for a long, painful talk. We both agreed to see a marriage counselor. I told Tracy that if Ally turned out to be his child, then I would support his decision to take part in her life. In fact, over the past week and a half, I had come to terms with the idea of Ally belonging to Tracy.

I had accepted it, and even felt a fluttering of excitement at the thought of seeing her again. You might be shocked, I know, but you have to remember that I spent a lot of time with Ally.

The DNA tests came back. Phylicia, a very subdued Drew, Lee, and a very angry Sloan met at our house to find out the results. At our request, the lab tech had written the results and sealed the contents in an envelope.

Without a doubt, I was the calmest person in the group. Sloan was crying again, even before the results were read. Phyllis and Drew sat together, but they both looked pale and anxious.

Was I the only one that wouldn't mind if Tracy turned out to be Ally's father? And what if it turned out to be Phyllis and Drew? Amber might no longer blame them for Sloan Kelly's death, but the relationship between her and Phyllis and Drew would probably always be rocky at best.

What kind of life would Ally have with that type of tension?

The six of us stared at the envelope on the coffee table for a long moment before Phyllis finally stirred. "I guess if nobody else will do it, I will." She picked up the envelope, tore it open, and unfolded the lab report.

I don't think anyone was breathing. I knew that I wasn't.

Finally, Phyllis looked up.

At Lee, then Sloan. I saw Phyllis wince visibly as she said dully, "Lee, you're a match."

"God," Sloan moaned. She pushed Lee aside and raced into the kitchen.

I followed, unaccountably disappointed. If only Tracy had been a match, I thought as I reached Sloan and drew her against my shoulder. She cried, great, heartbreaking sobs.

After a few moments, she lifted her head and looked at me. Her face and her expression were a pitiful sight, her voice thick with agony.

"I—I wanted to be the one to have Lee's baby, Samantha!"

"I know, Sloan, I know. But what's done is done. Do you still love Lee?" After a brief hesitation, she nodded. Tears continued to roll down her face. "Then work it out. Ally's a wonderful baby, and she's not to blame. You can have your own babies with Lee. If you have to, remind yourself every day that if Lee hadn't been drugged, then he might not have done what he did."

"Is—is that what you're going to do?"

I nodded, then smiled ruefully. "Well, that and a marriage counselor."

A glimmer of hope lit her eyes. "Maybe we could go as a group? I mean, we all went through this together. . . ."

Why not? I thought. Sloan was right, we had gone through this together. "I'll talk to the others about it, okay?"

And that's what we did. In the end, Sloan and Lee agreed to help Amber financially, and eventually Sloan began keeping Ally some while Amber worked.

Amazingly, none of the couples got divorced, but Phyllis and Drew sold their house and moved away. I think that might have been the best thing for them, to get away from the constant reminders.

I still get to see Ally, and Tracy and I are expecting our first baby, finally.

I hope she's a girl, and that she's as sweet as Ally.

THE END